# DOOMED on DEATH ROW



by Dee Phillips

illustrated by Anthony Resto

New York, New York

**Credits**
Cover, © Fer Gregory/Shutterstock, © Fresnel/Shutterstock, and © Katrina Elena/Shutterstock.

Publisher: Kenn Goin
Senior Editor: Joyce Tavolacci
Creative Director: Spencer Brinker

Library of Congress Cataloging-in-Publication Data in process at time of publication (2017)
Library of Congress Control Number: 2016018836
ISBN-13: 978-1-944102-35-7 (library binding)



For more information, write to Bearport Publishing Company, Inc., 45 West 21st Street, Suite 3B, New York, New York 10010.
Printed in the United States of America.

10 9 8 7 6 5 4 3 2 1

# Contents

# CHAPTER 1
# A Night in Prison

The cold, damp air smelled of **decay**. Slowly, Joe, his best friend Daniel, and a large group of their friends walked into the prison **cellblock**. The cells along the crumbling main corridor were framed with old, rusty bars. Water trickled down the walls, leaving slimy stains and puddles on the stone floor. Every footstep the boys took echoed in the eerie silence.

*Bang!* An ear-splitting noise cut through the silence. Some of the boys jumped as the heavy doors of the prison slammed shut behind them.

A tall, **burly** prison officer stepped from the shadows. "Welcome to Batley Prison," he growled. "This is the home of the state's most **notorious** criminals."

The officer jangled a big bunch of keys. "My name is Warden Mark Smith. You are now all prison **inmates**."

Warden Smith stepped closer to the boys and lowered his voice. "Do not be surprised if you hear cries after dark. Many men lived out their final days in these cells, and their unhappy spirits haunt the prison."

The boys looked at each other nervously.

Then, Warden Smith's expression changed completely. He smiled and gave a big, hearty chuckle. "But that shouldn't stop you from having a great Halloween, boys!" he shouted. "Think of how lucky you are to be spending Halloween night in this old, **abandoned** prison."

The boys nervousness immediately vanished, and they all cheered.

As the boys excitedly set down their backpacks, Joe smiled at Warden Smith. He knew the warden by a different name, Uncle Mark. Joe's uncle wasn't really a prison warden. In real life, he was the **curator** of the **historic** prison, and he dressed up as a prison officer to give people tours. When Uncle Mark suggested that Joe bring a group of friends to the spooky old prison for Halloween, Joe was thrilled.

After the boys unrolled their sleeping bags, they set off on a tour. Uncle Mark led them down a long, narrow corridor that stretched the length of the cellblock. As they walked, he explained that the prison had been closed for nearly fifty years. Once, however, it had been home to hundreds of inmates.

Joe and Daniel peered into one of the cells. The only light came from a tiny window with bars on it. The **dilapidated** metal frame of a bed stood against one wall, filling almost half the cell.

"Look," said Daniel, pointing to a wall. Someone had scratched forty-five tally marks into it.

Joe wondered if the prisoner had lived in the tiny cell for forty-five days . . . or forty-five years?

At the end of the cellblock, Uncle Mark unlocked a thick metal door. "Okay, boys," he said. "You are now entering

what's known as death row. Prisoners who were to be **executed** spent their final days in these cells."

Without saying a word, the group of boys followed Joe's uncle through the door. Even though the death row cells had stood empty for decades, the stale, cold air still seemed heavy with **melancholy** and dread. In silence, the boys spread out to explore the creepy building.

At the end of the row of cells was another door, standing slightly open. Joe and Daniel crept away from their friends and peeked through the crack in the door.

Behind the door was a small room with a high ceiling. In the center of the room was a set of wooden steps that led up to a platform. Both boys let out a small gasp as they noticed a **noose** dangling from a **gallows** on top of the platform.

Joe and Daniel knew they shouldn't be in that room and quickly rejoined the group.

"Take a look around the cellblock, or you can visit the prison cemetery. That's where inmates who were executed are buried," said Uncle Mark. "I want everyone back here in fifteen minutes."

"Come on," said Daniel to Joe. "I want to see the cemetery."

As Joe followed Daniel outside, shivers ran down his spine. No matter how hard he tried, he couldn't stop thinking about the old, **tattered** noose.

## CHAPTER 2

# The Black Dog

The daylight was starting to fade as Joe and Daniel walked out of the building toward the cemetery.

Joe looked up at the high brick wall that surrounded the prison. On top of the wall, **silhouetted** against the darkening sky, were coils of barbed wire. There was also a huge metal gate—the only way in or out of the prison—topped with metal spikes.

Joe and Daniel walked between the rows of old tombstones. At the end of one row, Daniel tripped on a thick vine and tumbled to the ground. He fell against a tombstone with "Carter 8355" written on it. As Joe helped Daniel untangle the thorny vine from around his feet, the boys heard a low snarling sound.

A huge, black dog was crouching just a few feet from them. Its ears were flat against its head and the fur on its back stood on end. It looked as if it was trying to protect something.

"Easy, boy," said Daniel, in a shaky voice as he slowly stood up.

The dog's breath hung in the cool air like smoke.

"I have an idea," said Joe, reaching into his pocket. "Would you like something to eat, boy?" he asked, terrified.

Joe pulled out a granola bar and tossed it toward the dog's jaws. To the boys' horror, the granola bar seemed to pass straight through the dog's huge head, landing with a thud on the ground.

Slowly, the dog inched toward them . . .

Joe and Daniel each let out a loud scream.

All of a sudden, the boys heard Uncle Mark's voice. "What's going on? Is everything okay?" he asked.

"Be careful," whispered Joe over his shoulder. "There's a black dog and . . ." Joe suddenly stopped talking when he realized the dog had completely disappeared!

"Where did it go?" gasped Daniel, spinning around to look in every direction.

"It was just here!" cried Joe. "I threw it a granola bar, and then . . ." He hesitated, suddenly feeling very foolish.

Uncle Mark walked toward them and looked at the tombstone. "A dog, really?" he said. "Very strange. This is the grave of a prisoner named Jackson Carter who died a long time ago. He once had a dog. . . ."

"Really? What happened to him?" Joe asked.

As Uncle Mark led Joe and Daniel back toward the cellblock, he told them the story.

"Jackson Carter was **convicted** of murdering his brother in 1931 and was sentenced to death. Carter had a big black dog. The story goes that the dog came to the prison gates every day and waited there, howling. After Carter was executed, he was buried in the cemetery. One day, the dog found its way into the cemetery and began guarding Carter's grave. The prison

officers tried to chase the animal away, but it refused to leave."

"So, what happened to the dog?" asked Daniel.

Warden Smith stopped walking and turned to look back at the graves that were now covered in heavy mist.

"Eventually the poor creature died of old age," he said. "The prison officers took **pity** on the loyal animal and buried it next to Carter."

Joe and Daniel couldn't believe what they were hearing.

"Do you think we saw Carter's dog, Uncle Mark?" asked Joe.

His uncle chuckled. "I can't say, boys," he said. "Over the years, people have seen some pretty strange things around here."

"Come on," he said, turning back toward the prison building. "It's time for you kids to get something to eat."

Once inside, Uncle Mark lit a lantern in one of the prison cells and handed out cups of hot pumpkin soup. Soon the boys were huddled in their sleeping bags enjoying their soup and telling ghost stories.

Daniel and Joe didn't feel much like joining in with the Halloween fun, though. As they curled up in their sleeping bags, both boys were thinking about the ghostly dog.

Joe jolted awake from a deep sleep. For just a moment, he wasn't sure where he was. Then, he remembered he was at the old prison. Joe's watch showed it was 11:15 P.M.

As Joe closed his eyes to go back to sleep, he realized he could hear a heavy panting sound. He peered into the darkness. At the end of his sleeping bag, just inches from his feet, stood the big black dog.

Terrified, Joe didn't dare make a move. The dog stared hard at Joe—its intense brown eyes appeared to glow. Then it turned away and trotted out into the corridor. The dog slowly returned and stood again at the end of Joe's sleeping bag.

Joe reached out his arm and gently shook Daniel.

"Wake up, Dan," he whispered. "The black dog is here! It's watching us."

Bleary-eyed, Daniel raised himself up on his elbows and followed Joe's gaze.

The big black dog steadily returned the boys' stares. Then, once again, it trotted out into the corridor.

"I think it wants us to follow it," said a confused Joe.

"Are you crazy?" hissed Daniel. "I'm not following that dog anywhere."

"Come on," said Joe. "I think it really wants to show us something."

Joe scrambled from his sleeping bag, pulled on his sneakers, and grabbed a flashlight. Daniel reluctantly followed, and the two boys crept away from their group of friends.

The dog waited for the boys and then slowly trotted off into the shadows. Their hearts thumping, Joe and Daniel followed the big animal, trying hard not to look into the pitch-black cells on either side.

At the end of the corridor, they reached the door that led to death row. The boys watched as the dog simply passed through the door and disappeared from view.

“I’m not going in there,” said Daniel, his voice trembling.

Joe didn’t feel much braver than his friend. Finally, he said, “Come on. We have to find out what the dog wants.”

Together, the boys pulled open the heavy door and stepped into the cold darkness of death row.

CHAPTER 3

# Doomed on Death Row

The boys trembled with fear as they followed the ghostly creature past the cells. Then, about halfway along the cellblock, the dog walked into one of the cells—passing straight through the thick metal bars. The boys edged toward the bars, squinting into the inky darkness.

Sitting on a rusty old bunk bed, the boys could make out the hunched shape of a man. He appeared to be dressed in a blue-and-white striped prison uniform with a small cap perched on his head.

The dog walked toward the man and lay down at his feet. Then it rested its snout on the man's foot and closed its eyes. The man reached a big rough hand down toward the dog and stroked its fur. Then he turned to look at the boys. Getting stiffly to his feet, he staggered toward the bars of the cell.

Joe had never seen a face that showed such misery. He guessed the man was in his twenties, but the black circles beneath his **haggard** eyes and his hollow cheeks made him look much older.

"What do you want?" growled the man. His voice was **hoarse** as if he'd not spoken for a very long time.

Joe and Daniel looked at each other in utter confusion. How could there still be a prisoner on death row when the prison has been closed for so many years?

"I said, what do you want?" roared the prisoner, grabbing the bars of his cell and shaking them hard.

Joe's stomach was doing somersaults.

"We, we . . . followed your dog . . . sir," he stuttered. "It led us here."

"Pah," hissed the prisoner.

There was a question buzzing in Joe's head. Finally, he got up the courage to ask, "Are . . . are . . . you Jackson Carter, sir?"

The prisoner's fingers tightened around the metal bars. "That's me," he said. "Jackson Carter, Prisoner 8355. **Condemned** to death for the murder of my brother."

"Got any more questions?" he snarled into Joe's face.

Joe and Daniel backed away from the bars, hardly able to believe they were face-to-face with a ghostly murderer.

But then, as if all the energy had drained from his body, Carter's head drooped forward. With his hands still clinging to the bars, his shoulders began to shake as huge sobs overcame his body.

"I didn't do it . . ." he howled. "I promise you kid, I'm innocent!"

Joe crept back toward the bars and quietly asked, "What happened, Mr. Carter? How did you end up here?"

Carter rubbed his hand wearily across his eyes.

"My older brother, Ellis, and I never got on. He could do no wrong in our father's eyes. He was handsome and smart. Everybody loved Ellis. Me?" Carter hesitated. "I was the **outcast** of the family. Nobody liked me."

Carter gave a big sad sigh. "The only person who ever really loved me was our little sister, Mari. She had the brightest yellow hair you'd ever seen. My little Lady Marigold I used to call her. All day, she'd follow me around."

Carter slowly shuffled back to his bunk and slumped down onto it. Then he continued his story. "As our father got older, he told everyone he wanted Ellis to take over our farm. That was fine by me. I liked caring for the animals, but I was no businessman."

"Then it happened. . . ." A sob seemed to catch in Carter's throat.

"Ellis and I were working in the **hayloft** one afternoon. We had an argument, and he called me a name. I got mad, I admit it. But I never thought he'd take a step back."

Carter's voice was little more than a whisper. "He fell from the hayloft."

Carter turned his face to the cold, damp wall. "I climbed down to help him, but it was too late. He'd cracked his skull. Poor little Mari came into the barn and found me holding our brother. I was covered in his blood."

Carter turned to look at the boys, his eyes burned with anger. "After that, there was nothing I could do or say. They all believed I'd killed him—even though it was an accident. They said I'd done it so I would **inherit** the farm."

Suddenly, the big black dog stood up. The fur on its back bristled and a low growl rumbled in its throat.

In the distance, Joe and Daniel heard the sound of footsteps and rattling keys.

Carter stood up, too. “It's nearly midnight,” he said. “They're coming for me.”

“What do you mean?” asked Joe. “Who's coming for you?”

“The guards,” said Carter. “Every night they come for me. Every night for the past eighty-five years. They'll lead me to the gallows. At one minute past midnight, I'll be hanged. I have relived the terrible last night of my life over and over and over again.”

Joe felt a knot of fear and panic form under his ribs. "Can't you escape?" he asked. "Just walk through the bars of your cell . . . like your dog."

Carter shook his head sadly. "It's not possible," he said. "I have tried to escape, but I believe my spirit is trapped here."

The big dog growled again. As the boys watched in horror, four prison officers appeared from the shadows and walked stiffly toward Carter's cell.

Carter looked into Joe's eyes. "If I could just tell my little Lady Marigold what happened, I believe I could rest in peace."

The ghostly prison guards didn't seem to notice Joe and Daniel. One of the men unlocked the bars of Carter's cell. Then, in a loud, clear voice he said, "Jackson Carter, you have been convicted of the murder of Ellis Carter. It's time for your execution."

Joe held back tears as he watched Carter shuffle from the cell. Surrounded by the guards, Carter walked slowly toward the room where the boys had seen the gallows.

The big black dog left the cell and followed. At the end of the corridor, the group seemed to melt into the door like mist.

The boys waited, unsure what to do next. Finally, Joe looked at his watch. It was one minute past midnight.

# CHAPTER 4
# Lady Marigold Carter

Daniel and Joe crept back through the dark prison and climbed into their sleeping bags. For the rest of the night, all Joe could do was think about poor Jackson Carter, doomed to be a prisoner on death row forever.

By morning, Joe and Daniel had decided to tell Uncle Mark everything.

As Joe, Daniel, and Uncle Mark drove home from the prison sleepover, Joe said to Uncle Mark, "Please don't be mad, but last night Daniel and I went back to death row . . . and we saw something. We saw Jackson Carter!"

Then Joe and Daniel described everything that had happened. At first Uncle Mark was silent. Then the expression on his face grew serious. "I don't know what to say, boys," he said.

"Please, Uncle Mark, you've got to believe us," said Joe.

Uncle Mark thought of something that might comfort the boys. "Miss Mari Carter still lives in this town. She's a very old lady now, but you could tell her what happened," Uncle Mark said.

The next day, Joe, Daniel, and Uncle Mark were squeezed onto Miss Carter's tiny sofa in her living room. Nervously, the boys told her their story.

Miss Carter listened to the boys, occasionally wiping a tear from her eyes. When the story was finished, she said, "Thank you for coming here, boys. I've wanted to believe my dear Jackson was innocent for eighty-five years, but . . . I'm much too old to believe in ghosts." Then she smiled kindly.

An image of Jackson Carter's anguished face suddenly flashed in Joe's mind.

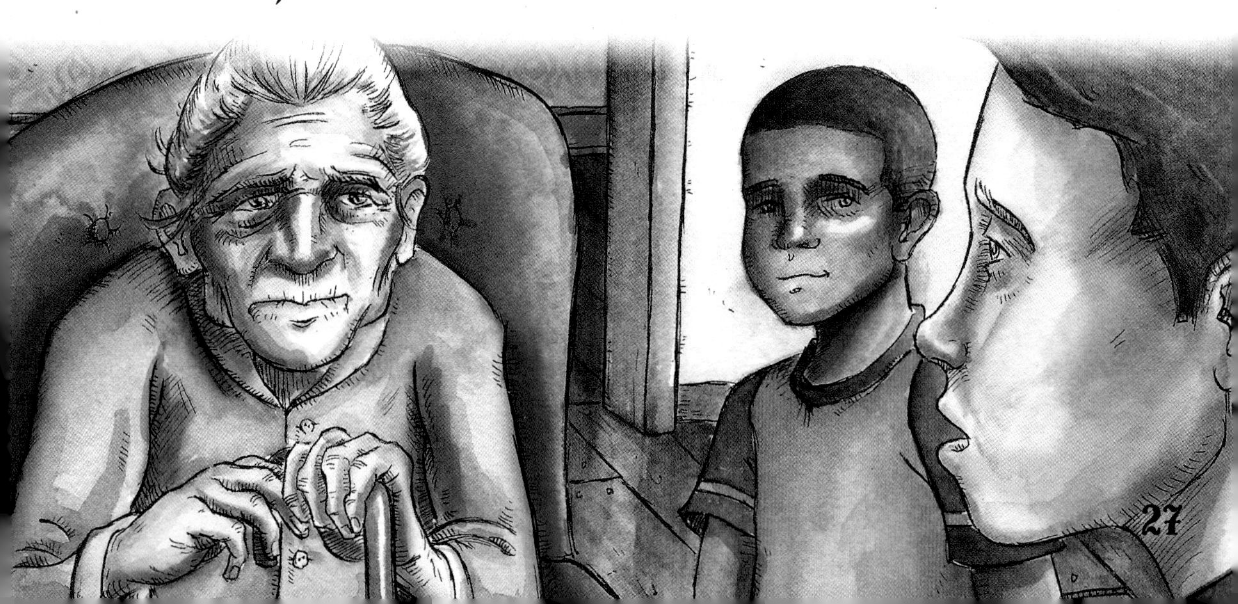

"I promise you it's true, ma'am," he pleaded. "The last thing Mr. Carter said to us was: *If I could just tell my little Lady Marigold what happened, I believe I could rest in peace.*"

As the words left Joe's lips, Miss Carter's thin, wrinkled hands began to shake, rattling the teacup and saucer she held. "What did you say, dear? Did you say *Lady Marigold*?" she asked.

Both boys quickly nodded.

"Oh my goodness," she gasped. "That was Jackson's special name for me. It was our secret."

A huge smile lit up Miss Carter's face. "There's only one way these boys could have known that nickname . . ." she said. "My own dear brother must have told them."

An hour later, as Uncle Mark waited in the car, Joe and Daniel made their way across the prison cemetery.

Miss Carter had asked the boys if they'd do one thing for her. In his hands, Joe carried a small bag of marigold seeds from Miss Carter's garden.

Joe and Daniel knelt down in front of Jackson Carter's tombstone, and Joe carefully sprinkled the seeds onto the ground.

"Look!" whispered Daniel to Joe.

Nearby, a big black dog and a young man wearing a striped jacket and pants were watching the boys. After a few seconds, the shadowy figures turned away and headed toward the prison gates. As if the thick metal bars of the gate did not exist, the ghostly figures simply walked through the bars and left the prison behind . . . forever.

# Doomed on Death Row

1. Why are Joe, Daniel, and their friends spending the night in Batley Prison?

2. Which two characters from the story are buried in the prison cemetery?

3. What convinces Joe and Daniel that the black dog is a ghost? Use examples from the story to explain your thoughts.

4. How do you think Carter is feeling in this scene?

5. Why does Mari Carter eventually believe Joe and Daniel's story?

**abandoned** (uh-BAN-duhnd) no longer in use

**burly** (BUR-lee) large in size

**cellblock** (SEL-blok) a unit in a prison made up of many small rooms

**condemned** (KUHN-demd) declared guilty

**convicted** (kon-VIK-tid) found guilty of a crime

**curator** (KYOO-ray-tur) a person in charge of a museum

**decay** (di-KAY) rotting matter

**dilapidated** (dih-LAP-i-day-tid) fallen into ruin

**executed** (EK-suh-*kyoo*-tid) put to death

**gallows** (GAL-ohz) a wooden frame used to hang people

**haggard** (HAG-urd) looking exhausted or unwell

**hayloft** (HEY-lawft) a place in a barn where hay is stored

**historic** (hiss-TOR-ik) dating from the past

**hoarse** (HORSS) having a voice that sounds rough and harsh

**inherit** (in-HERR-uht) to receive something from someone who has died

**inmates** (IN-mayts) prisoners

**melancholy** (mel-uhn-KOHL-ee) a feeling of deep sadness

**noose** (NOOSS) a loop made of rope used to hang people

**notorious** (noh-TOR-ee-uhs) being well known for something bad

**outcast** (OUT-kast) a person who is rejected by a group

**pity** (PIT-ee) the feeling of sorrow for another person

**silhouetted** (si-loo-ET-uhd) shown the dark shape and outline of something

**tattered** (TAT-urd) old and torn

## ABOUT THE AUTHOR

Dee Phillips develops and writes nonfiction books for young readers and fiction books—including historical fiction—for middle graders and young adults. She loves to read and write stories that have a twist or an unexpected, thought-provoking ending. Dee lives near the ocean on the southwest coast of England. A keen hiker, her biggest ambition is to one day walk the entire coast of Great Britain.

## ABOUT THE ILLUSTRATOR

Anthony Resto graduated from the American Academy of Art with a BFA in Watercolor. He has been illustrating children's books, novellas, and comics for six years, and is currently writing his own children's book. His most recent illustrated books include *Happyland: A Tale in Two Parts* and *Oracle of the Flying Badger*. You can find his other illustrated books and fine art works at anthonyresto.com. In his free time, he enjoys restoring his vintage RV and preparing for the zombie apocalypse.